TO KAREN DANNEWITZ AND THE DANVILLE COMMUNITY PRESBYTERIAN PRESCHOOL TEACHERS
—S. M. E.

FOR JODI
—D. S.

Text copyright © 2012 by Susan Middleton Elya
Illustrations copyright © 2012 by Dan Santat

First published in the United States of America in April 2012
by Bloomsbury Children's Books
www.bloomsbury.com

Bloomsbury is a registered trademark of Bloomsbury Publishing Plc

For information about permission to reproduce selections from this book, write to
Permissions, Bloomsbury Children's Books, 1385 Broadway, New York, New York 10018
Bloomsbury books may be purchased for business or promotional use. For information on bulk
purchases please contact Macmillan Corporate and Premium Sales Department at
specialmarkets@macmillan.com

Library of Congress Cataloging-in-Publication Data
Elya, Susan Middleton.
Fire! ¡Fuego! Brave bomberos / by Susan Elya ; illustrated by Dan Santat. — 1st U.S. ed.
p.   cm.
Summary: A brave group of firefighters set off to battle a blaze at a town house.
Spanish words interspersed in the rhyming text are defined in a glossary.
ISBN 978-1-59990-461-0 (hardcover) • ISBN 978-1-59990-759-8 (reinforced)
[1. Stories in rhyme. 2. Fire fighters—Fiction.] I. Santat, Dan, ill. II. Title. III. Title: ¡Fuego! Brave bomberos.
PZ8.3.E514Fir 2012   [E]—dc22   2011004934

Art created with colored pencil, water on ink print, fire, and Photoshop
Typeset in Avenir Lt Std
Book design by Regina Roff
Printed in China by C&C Offset Printing Co., Ltd., Shenzhen, Guangdong
(hardcover) 10 9 8 7
(reinforced) 10 9 8 7 6 5 4 3 2 1

FIRE! ¡FUEGO!

FIRE
RESCUE

BRAVE BOMBEROS

Susan Middleton Elya ★ illustrated by Dan Santat

BLOOMSBURY

NEW YORK LONDON OXFORD NEW DELHI SYDNEY

Brave **bomberos**, our protectors,
Juan, **José**, **Carlota**, **Héctor**.

At the station, sirens sound.

Corazones start to pound.

"House fire!" says **el capitán**.

"**¡Fuego!** Get your helmets on!"

Down the pole, they grab their gear.

¡RAPIDO! WE'RE OUT OF HERE!

Helmets on, **abrigos**, **botas**.

"Hurry!" bark their loyal **mascotas**.

Out they go! The rig is ready.
Climb aboard and hold on steady.
Héctor drives; the captain rides.
The other three hang off the sides.
Hold on tight to make the turn,
round the corner, smell the burn!

Air is crackly, hot and dry.
Gray-black **humo** fills the sky.
Brave **bomberos**, twitching noses,
stop the truck and lug their hoses,
point the heavy, huge **manguera**,
spray the town house, all **madera**.

Hydrant on, the water flows;
ten strong hands to brace the hose.
Aim **el agua**, hear the sizzle—
soon they make **las flamas** fizzle.

People watch, both friend and neighbor.
All stay back to see them labor.
Douse those ashes just in case—
grit and sweat on every face!

Scary work deserves respect.

¿Peligroso? That's correct!

Captain bellows, "Building's clear!"

But what's that tiny noise they hear?

Through a window, faint *meow*.
Need to save that **gato**! How?

Firemen raise the ladder high.

I'LL GO. I'LL GO.

LET ME TRY!

HEY, COMPADRES, MOMENTITO! LET ME SAVE THAT POOR GATITO.

Climbing up **la escalera**,

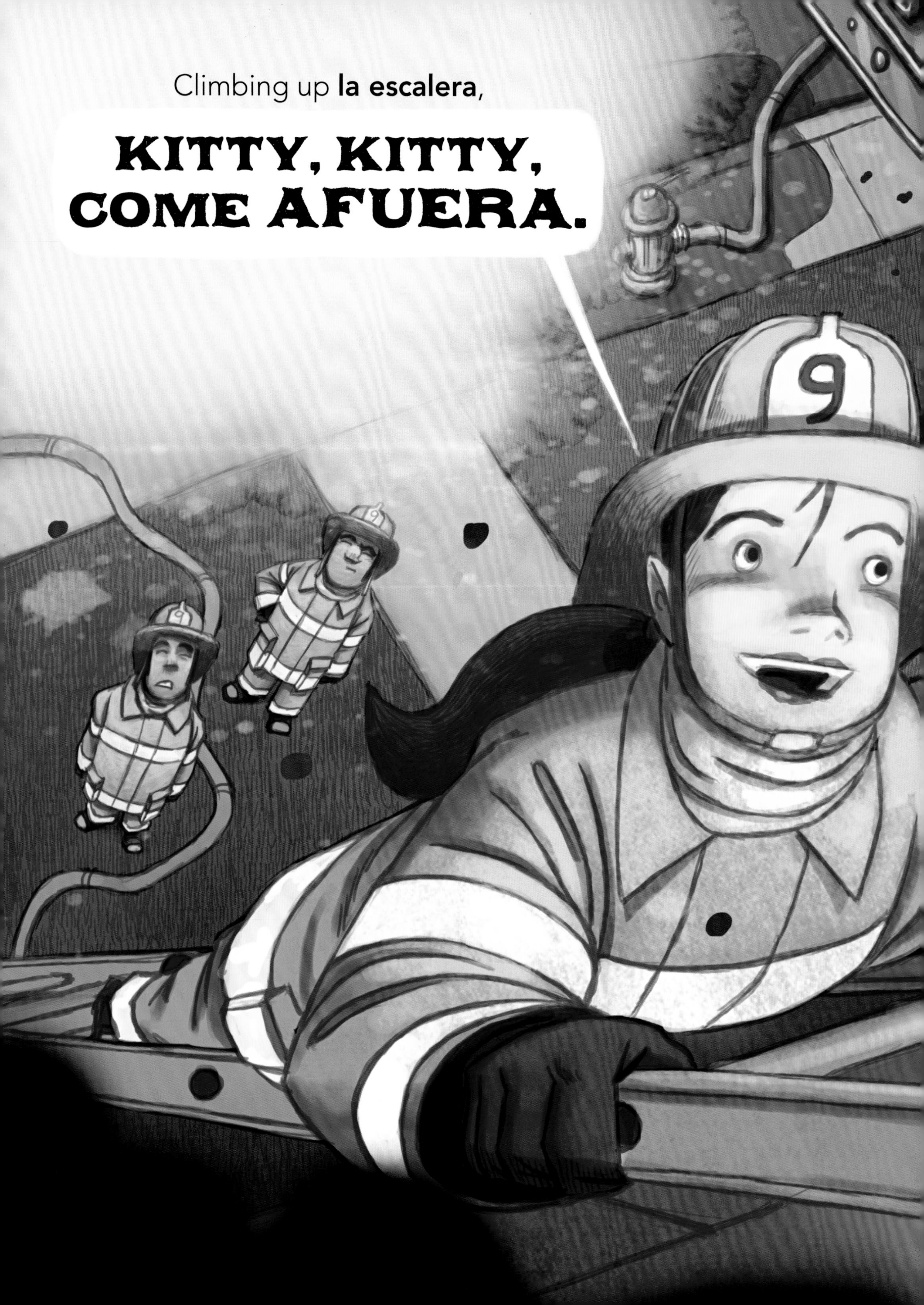

Coaxed by food in small **pedazos**,
kitten jumps to outstretched **brazos**.

Gato safely on the ground,
kitty **besos** all around.
"You're our hero!" cheer **los niños**
as they give the cat **cariños**.
Says **Carlota**, caked with grime,

AT YOUR SERVICE, ANY TIME.

"Thanks, **bomberos**," people cheer.

GLAD TO KNOW YOU GUYS ARE HERE.

Juan says, "Safety, that's our goal."
Héctor adds, "Stop, drop, and roll!"

Crowd disperses, one by one.

Fire extinguished; work is done.

Embers cold—no need to stay.

"Time for dinner!" shouts **José**.

Capitán, his hunger big,

says, "Pack the hoses! Board the rig!"

Brave **bomberos** reach their station,
time for rest and relaxation,
eat their supper, wash **los platos**,
feed the pets—**los perros**, **gatos**.

Just as **todos** drift to sleep,
Dispatch makes its noisy bleep.
Late-night fire call has begun.

¡E-MER-GEN

Off they go to fight **un fuego**—
brave **bomberos**.
¡Hasta luego!

 GLOSSARY

abrigos (ah BREE goce): coats

afuera (ah FWEH rah): outside

agua (AH gwah): water

besos (BEH soce): kisses

bomberos (bome BEH roce): firefighters

botas (BOE tahs): boots

brazos (BRAH soce): arms

capitán (kah pee TAHN): captain

cariños (kah REE nyoce): affection

Carlota (kahr LOE tah): Carla

casa (KAH sah): house

compadres (kohm PAH drehs): comrades, coworkers

corazones (koe rah SOE nehs): hearts

el (ehl): the

emergencia (eh mehr HEHN syah): emergency

escalera (ehs kah LEH rah): ladder

flamas (FLAH mahs): flames

fuego (FWEH goe): fire

gatito (gah TEE toe): kitten

gato (GAH toe): cat

hasta luego (AHS tah LWEH goe): see you later

Héctor (EHK tohr): Hector

humo (OO moe): smoke

José (hoe SEH): Joe

Juan (HWAHN): John

la, las, los (LAH, LAHS, LOCE): the

madera (mah DEH rah): wood

manguera (mahn GHEH rah): hose

mascotas (mahs KOE tahs): pets

momentito (moe mehn TEE toe): a moment, please

niños (NEE nyoce): children

pedazos (peh DAH soce): pieces

peligroso (peh lee GROE soe): dangerous

perros (PEH rroce): dogs

platos (PLAH toce): dishes

rápido (RRAH pee doe): quickly

todos (TOE doce): all

un (OON): a, an